VIKING
Published by the Penguin Group
Viking Penguin, a division of Penguin Books USA Inc.,
375 Hudson Street, New York, New York 10014, U.S.A.
Penguin Books Ltd, 27 Wrights Lane, London W8 5TZ, England
Penguin Books Australia Ltd, Ringwood, Victoria, Australia
Penguin Books Canada Ltd, 10 Alcorn Avenue, Toronto, Ontario, Canada M4V 3B2
Penguin Books (N.Z.) Ltd, 182–190 Wairau Road, Auckland 10, New Zealand

Penguin Books Ltd, Registered Offices: Harmondsworth, Middlesex, England

First published in 1992 by Viking Penguin, a division of Penguin Books USA Inc.
A Vanessa Hamilton Book
Produced in association with Gyldendal, Copenhagen

1   3   5   7   9   10   8   6   4   2

Text copyright © Margaret Mahy, 1992
Illustrations copyright © Patricia MacCarthy, 1992
All rights reserved

ISBN 0-670-84547-7
Library of Congress catalog card number: 91-67694

Printed in Portugal

MARGARET MAHY

THE HORRENDOUS HULLABALOO

Illustrated by Patricia MacCarthy

Viking

There was once a cheerful old woman who kept house for her nephew, Peregrine – a pirate by profession.

Every morning she put on her pirate pinafore, poured out Peregrine's ration of rum, picked up his socks, and petted his parrot. She worked day in, day out, keeping everything shipshape.

Meanwhile, her pirate nephew went out to parties every night, though he never once asked his aunt or his parrot if they would like to go with him.

Whenever his aunt suggested that she and the parrot might want to come too, Peregrine replied, "You wouldn't enjoy pirate parties, dear aunt. The hullabaloo is horrendous!"

"But I like horrendous hullabaloos!" exclaimed the aunt. "And so does the parrot."

"When I come home from sea I want a break from the parrot," said Peregrine, looking proud and piratical. "And if I took my aunt to a party, all the other pirates would laugh at me."

"Very well," thought his aunt, "I shall have a party of my own."

Without further ado she sent out dozens of invitations written in gold ink. Then she baked batch after batch of delicious rumblebumpkins while the parrot hung upside down on a plant, clacking its beak greedily.

No sooner had Peregrine set off that evening on another night's hullabaloo than his aunt, shutting the door behind him, peeled off her pirate pinafore and put on her patchwork party dress.

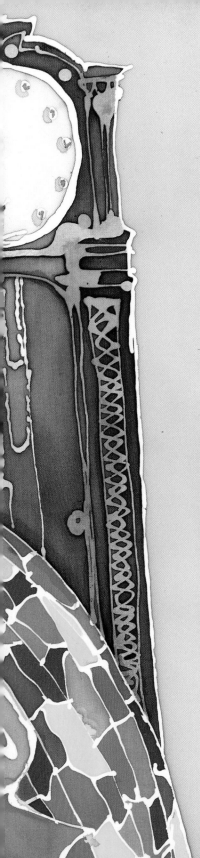

"Half past seven!" she called to the parrot. "We'll soon be having a horrendous hullabaloo of our own!"

Then she opened the windows and sat waiting for the guests to come, enjoying the salty scent of the sea, and the sound of the waves washing around Peregrine's pirate ship, out in the moonlit bay.

"Half past eight!" chimed the clock. The pirate's aunt waited.

"Half past nine!" chimed the clock. The pirate's aunt still waited, shuffling her feet and tapping her fingers.

"Half past ten!" chimed the clock. The rumblebumpkins were in danger of burning. No one, it seemed, was brave enough to come to a party at a pirate's house. The pirate's aunt shed bitter tears over the rumblebumpkins.

Suddenly the parrot spoke.
"I have lots of friends who love
rumblebumpkins," she cackled.
"Friends who aren't plunged into
panic or petrified by pirates –
friends who would happily help
with a hullabaloo!"

"Well, what are you waiting
for?" cried the pirate's aunt. "Go
and get them at once!"

Out of the window the parrot
flew, while the aunt mopped
up her tears and
patted powder on
her nose.

Almost at once the night air was filled with flapping and fluttering. The sea swished and sighed. The night breeze smelled of passion fruit, pineapples and palm trees. In through the open windows tumbled the patchwork party guests, all screeching with laughter. They were speckled, they were freckled; they were streaked and striped like rollicking rags of rainbow. All the parrots in town had come to the aunt's party.

"Come one, come all!" the aunt cried happily.

The parrots cackled loudly, breaking into a spirited singsong. So loud was the singsong that the pirate's neighbors rushed out of their houses, prepared for the worst.

"What a horrendous hullabaloo!" they cried in amazement.

The aunt invited them all to feast richly on her rumblebumpkins, and to join her in a wild jig. She was having a wonderful time.

When Peregrine arrived home later that night, his house was still ringing with leftover echoes of a horrendous hullabaloo. The air smelled strongly of rumblebumpkins, and the floor was covered in parrot feathers.

"Aunt!" he called crossly. "Come and tidy up at once."

But there was no one at home, for at that very moment, his aunt, still wearing her patchwork party dress, was stealing away on Peregrine's own pirate ship.

Over the moonlit sea she was sailing, with parrots perched all over her, making a horrendous hullabaloo. As they sailed off in search of passion fruit, pineapples and palm trees, it was impossible to tell where the aunt left off and the parrots began.

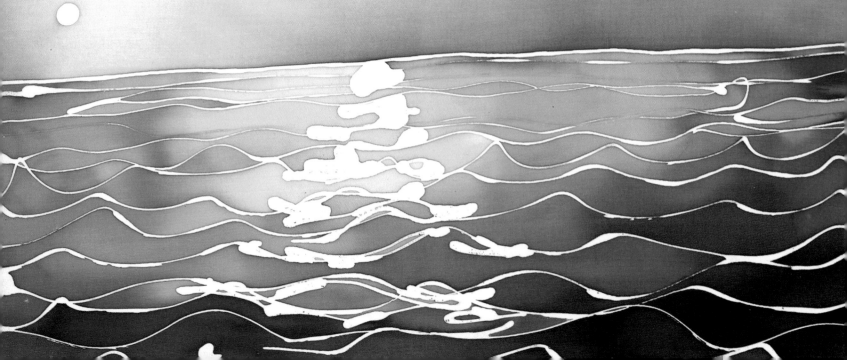

So, left all alone, with a grunt and a groan
Peregrine put on the pirate pinafore and tidied up
for himself.